Rose's Garden

Written by
Shauntae' E. Harris

Illustrated by
Ariel Anastasio

AuthorHouse™
1663 Liberty Drive
Bloomington, IN 47403
www.authorhouse.com
Phone: 1-800-839-8640

Script quotations are taken from the King James Version (KJV) of the Bible-Public Domain.

Published by AuthorHouse 02/14/2013

ISBN: 978-1-4817-1010-7 (sc)

Any people depicted in stock imagery provided by Thinkstock are models,
and such images are being used for illustrative purposes only.
Certain stock imagery © Thinkstock.

This book is printed on acid-free paper.

authorHOUSE®

This book is dedicated to all the little boys and girls who fall victim to bullying. You are beautifully and wonderfully made.

To the little bumblebee who feels low self–esteem or no hope—you are so much more than your fears. You were created in God's image and created in love.

To my two boys—I love you so much. I can't show you how to be men, but I can wrap you in love. You were created in greatness.

Acknowledgments

Special thanks to my mother for pushing me to stay on task, to Lady Shaunte' and Mrs. Torazzi Hayslett for taking the time to edit my book, and to a host of family and friends. Thank you for your love and support. It's greatly appreciated.

Once upon a time, far away in Hooverville, where God would send his angels to watch over all the boys and girls, lived a sweet but fearful young girl name Rose. She was a returning student at Hoover Elementary but refused to go to school. For the past two years, the kids had been making fun of Rose. They called her ugly and put glue in her hair. So this year, Rose was determined not to go.

It was early on a Monday morning,
and with the bright sun came the first
day of school.

"Come on, honey," Rose's mom called. "You're upset about last year, but I promise, you're going to have a great time. Rose, you're smart, and you're officially a fifth grader, my sweet bumblebee."

"Mom, please don't call me that," Rose replied.

"Well, honey, I'm sorry, but I'm sure this year will be different."

Rose wouldn't move. "I don't want to go. The kids hate me."

"Oh no, honey," her mom reassured her. "You just have to give them a chance to like you. They will begin to see what a great person you are. Let's go!"

Rose took her mother's advice and started moving, but she wasn't happy about it.

When they arrived at the school, Rose's mom walked Rose straight to class. "Well, honey, here is your class. Have a good day."

As Rose opened the door, she was very upset. "Why must I be tortured for another year?" she mumbled. "I have no friends, but here I go."

Before Rose sat in her seat, she decided to run back and give it one last shot with Mom. "Mom ... Mom, wait! Okay, sweet Mommy with cherries on top, please, please take me back home with you. The kids here will be so mean. I don't belong here."

Rose's mom replied, "Oh, Rose, you're warm as the sun. I assure you that God will send his angels to watch over you."

Rose stood on her tippy-toes and hugged her mom, giving her one big squeeze. "Sweet Mommy with cherries on top," she said again, "you must know that is not true. I don't believe in such foolishness."

Rose's mom smiled and directed Rose back to class. As Rose sat in her assigned seat, she held tight to the chair. She noticed other children coming in and looked around to see if there were any familiar faces from last year, but she noticed no one.

The teacher started class. Rose continued to look around but still noticed no one familiar. So far, no one had cracked a joke or made fun of her, so Rose smiled and thought, *Maybe Mom was right. This will be a great day.*

After a few hours in the class—and with Rose still holding on to the chair for dear life—the teacher announced the class would join another class for arts and crafts. The whole class would go to Mrs. Hayslett's room. Rose was so excited; art was one of her favorite things to do. The teacher said, "Everyone, please follow me."

As Rose and her classmates arrived in Mrs. Hayslett's room, Rose noticed the other art teacher, Ms. Kane, from last year. She was bringing in a group of her kids for art as well.

Rose decided to take a seat, and as soon as she sat down, she heard a loud voice call her name. "Rose, is that you?"

Rose looked behind her, and whom did she see? Robbie Brown, the meanest kid in the whole school. He stuck his tongue at her and started throwing paper. Rose was so embarrassed. She mumbled, "I really wanted to do some artwork, but here we go."

As the kids were doing artwork, Rose was ready to dash home. Luckily for her, she was saved by the lunch bell.

At lunchtime, she hoped Robbie would eat lunch outside as all the kids usually did on a sunny school day. Outside at lunchtime, the bullies would steel other kids' lunches, so when Rose heard the teacher say it was time to line up, Rose was so frightened. She didn't want to be anywhere close to Robbie, so she waited and waited so she could be at the back of the line.

Later, as Rose made her way to her lunch table, she felt something strange. "So quiet in here," she mumbled. And then something hit her on the neck ... and then on the face. All of a sudden,

she saw all the kids staring at her and then saw that it was mean Robbie throwing food at her. Rose just stood there. She tried to keep walking and ignore the name-calling and noise, but for some reason, her body wouldn't allow

her to move. Yet mean Robbie wouldn't stop. "Look at her! She's ugly. Aw, ha, you look like a rainbow."

As Robbie threw food at Rose, the kids started to chant, "Food fight! Food fight!" Rose was their main target. After what seemed to be the entire lunch period, the principal, Mrs. Booker, announced over the loud speaker that anyone caught throwing food would meet her in the principal's office.

The school day was closing, but Rose had not had any lunch, and she had no friends. After the first day of fifth grade, Rose was not sure if she would ever come back, but she still had to walk home from school for the first time.

When the bell rang, all the kids were dismissed to go home. Rose was not sure if it was safe for her to walk home yet, so she waited until she didn't see any kids around. She lived only five blocks away, so she was convinced she would make it home before her mom left for the store.

After waiting and waiting, Rose started walking home from school. She was so hungry. She decided to eat her banana on the way home, because she hadn't had a chance at lunchtime.

While she was walking, she felt something hard hit her on the back. Rose looked behind her and yelled, "Oh, no!" There was Robbie and his friends, at it again, coming out the bushes. Rose screamed, "Why won't you stop?" But they began chasing Rose and calling her names. "Roses are red. Violets are blue. Look at ugly Rose. We're coming after you."

Rose ran as fast as she could, dropping her smashed banana and the lunch pail her mother had made for her. She was so scared that she fell down. The kids caught up with her, and they threw rocks at her and kicked Rose on the ground. "Ah-ha! Look at you now," the kids said. "Rose looks like a brown—headed clown."

Rose got up and ran straight to her house. She ran so fast that she

tripped as she ran past her mother and up the stairs.

"Rose, honey, how was your first day?" her mother asked. Rose did not respond, so Rose's mom went up the stairs and found poor Rose, crying her little eyes out. "Oh, my little bumblebee, what's wrong?"

Rose said in a cracking voice, "Mommy, I hate school, and the kids hate me. I never want to go there again."

"Now, now, honey, it will all work out."

Rose said, "How do you know? And what should I do?"

Rose's mom told Rose to stand up and wipe her tears away. So Rose stood up and wiped her tears away. Her mother gently touched Rose's face and said, "Rose, never allow anyone to make you feel fearful or push you around. Sometimes people see you as you see yourself."

Rose looked at her mother, very puzzled. She asked, "What do you mean?"

"Honey, stand tall and look at me," her mom said. So Rose stood tall, looking directly in her mother's face. "Well, Rose, what do you see?" her mom asked.

"I see you, Mom."

"No, honey, I mean, what do you really see in yourself?"

"I see brown hair, big lips, boney legs, spider eyelashes, and dirty brown skin, not to mention a kid with no friends."

Rose's mom looked at Rose. "Oh no, honey, you are so beautiful, so perfectly made, and shaped in the right way. Why can't you see that? Rose, when I was a little girl about your age, the kids would make fun of me also, but that was because I allowed them to do it. My mother would tell me to stand on my own two feet and pray. So now I'm telling you just what my mother told me:

Rose, stand on your own two feet and pray. Find a special place, Rose, and pray to God—for anything, honey."

Rose looked at her mother with excitement, as if she'd found the answer. "Okay, Mom, I will pray, but it's going to take a lot of prayer for those kids." Rose was so excited. After her mom left the room, she thought, *Hmm, where could I pray? Mom didn't say I have to pray in one spot.*

So Rose got right on it; she started looking for a prayer spot. She got a flashlight and went into her closet. She began to feel uncomfortable. "Too many shoes in the way." On her second try to find a prayer spot, Rose said, "I know—I will go under my bed." But the bed was too low.

So on the third try, Rose decided to run to the bathroom. She jumped in the bathtub, but she began sliding all over the place. Poor Rose frowned.

On the fourth try—Rose believed four was the magic number—she decided this had to be the perfect prayer spot. "This is it. This is it," said Rose eagerly. She ran to the basement, but there she found furry visitors instead. "Yuk! Spider! Spider!" Rose screamed loudly and ran out of the basement. She tried a couple more places but without success.

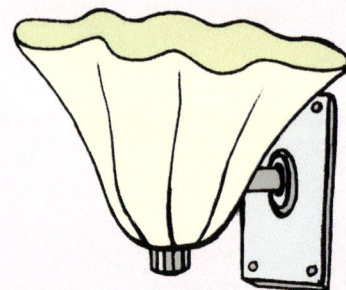

One day after school, Rose was looking out her window when she saw her family's garden. "I know! I know! This is it. This is really it," said Rose. It was Rose's seventh time looking for a prayer spot, and she was confident the garden would be the perfect spot. Rose ran out of her room and to the garden.

She was so excited about making the garden her prayer spot that she got on her knees and closed her eyes, but Rose didn't know how to pray. She opened one eye to see if she could get an idea, but nothing came to mind ... until Rose noticed a strange light shining from somewhere in the sky.

Rose looked around, but she didn't see anything, so she began to pray. "Dear God, can you please protect all the children from bullies, and please save them?"

Just as Rose was praying, she began to feel heat. So Rose looked down

but she saw nothing. Rose looked up, where the light was shining so brightly all around. Rose's skin started to glow, but poor Rose started to cry. She noticed the garden changing—it looked magical. Rose said, "God, can you make my color any color but brown and my eyes blue, so I don't have to frown? Can you take away my big lips and brown hair, so the kids will quit calling me a clown? I just want to be normal, so mean Robbie will stop pushing me around."

As Rose prayed, the sky begin to open, and Rose felt a tap on her shoulder. She opened her eyes and looked up. She saw the most beautiful thing she had ever seen. An angel had come from out of the sky. There were angels everywhere. The angel said in a whisper,

"Rose?" And Rose said, "Yes, I'm Rose." The angel said, "I have a message for you. Your prayer has been heard, and God is going to work it out in your favor." Rose started to smile and jump up and down. She said, "Yes! I'm going to be pink with blue eyes and black or blonde hair."

The angel smiled and said, "No, my child," and little Rose was confused.

Then Rose said in a whisper, "Are you the bully whisperer? I heard there were bully whisperers, and they would get rid of all the bad bullies."

The angel smiled again and said, "No, my child."

Rose said, "Then what do you mean, he works in my favor?"

The angel sat Rose down and told her, "When God created you, he created you in his own image. Because you are created in God's image, you can feel positive about yourself. Not liking yourself is saying that you don't like what God has made. God says, 'I'm Lord, and I give you power to believe you are special. Let no one take that away from you.' Rose, God looks on the inside, not the outside. You are beautiful, just the way God made you.

Everyone in the world was made in the image of God. If you have big lips, so what? God made them. Boney legs? So what? God made them. If you have slanted eyes or big eyes, so what? God made them too. Black, brown, or white skin? So what? God made you. Short, tall—God made them all. So thank him, Rose, for who you are."

As the angel was leaving, she gave Rose a special box. She said, "Remember this always from God: 'Be sure of this; I am with you always, even to the end of age.'"

Rose took the box and said, "I will keep this close to my heart, and please tell God thank you." As Rose watched the angel disappear far into the sky, it was already a new Rose who waved good–bye

On the next day of school, Rose opened the box. She was now considered a little angel from up top. Rose was so excited to show everyone the new her that before her mother could walk her to school, Rose was already out the house. She thanked God for her mother, and she thanked God for creating a beautiful her. She realized that if everyone were the same, the world would be boring. Because we are all different in our own way, that makes us all special.

When Rose arrived at school, she noticed Robbie was picking on another kid, so Rose walked straight to Robbie. "Look, you better stop bullying us kids, or I will tell the whole school about you wetting your pants last year. You don't have to bully or make people feel bad because you feel bad. So either you play nice, or don't play at all."

Robbie was shocked—no one had ever stood up to him, and because of that, he and Rose became friends. There was no more mean Robbie but best friend Robbie—and no more frowns from Rose being called a clown or from little Rose getting knocked on the ground. She kept her face lifted up to tell others that an angel had come down.

Although no one believed Rose, she knew what she had seen and that God had shown her to turn that frown around. After that, Rose smiled and had lots of friends all over town.

For it is God who works in you to will and to act in order to fulfill his good purpose.

—Philippians 2:13

Shauntae' E. Harris, is a mother of two. She was born and raised in Portland, Oregon. She started writing short stories, and plays, which was performed in local churches.Her creative vision, and wild imagination inspired many, so she decided to step out the box, and share with the world, how one individuals creativity can motivate millions. Being a single mother and true advocate for children's rights. She's hoping to help others take a stand in creating a positive atmosphere for children to be themselves and learn the power of prayer. Harris is a true believer in tackling issues that face children,and currently resides in San Diego California, with her boys. You may contact her at shauntaeharrisbooks@gmail.com

CPSIA information can be obtained
at www.ICGtesting.com
Printed in the USA
LVIC081323220413
330317LV00006B